This book belongs to...

Dedicated to Sora, Yume, Taye, Elle, Mashiro, Sakura, and all of their clouds.

— F.H.

Dedicated to Uta, the best song in my life.

— A.H.

Immedium, Inc.
P.O. Box 31846, San Francisco, CA 94131
www.immedium.com

First hardcover edition published 2011.

This book was typeset with Metallophile Sp8, handwritten felishino font, Meiryo, and HuiFont.
The illustrations were drawn on watercolor paper using ink, watercolor paint and pencils, markers, acrylic, and tissue paper collage.

Edited by Donn Menn
Book design by Felicia Hoshino

Printed in Singapore
10 9 8 7 6 5 4 3 2 1

Library of Congress Cataloging-in-Publication Data

Hoshino, Felicia.
    Sora and the cloud = Sora to kumo / by Felicia Hoshino. -- 1st hardcover ed.
      p. cm.
    Summary: A young boy climbs up a tree and into a waiting cloud, which takes him on a whirling adventure in the sky.
    ISBN 978-1-59702-027-5 (hardcover)
    [1. Clouds--Fiction. 2. Japanese language materials--Bilingual.] I. Title. II. Title: Sora to kumo.
    PZ49.31.H72 2011
    [E]--dc23

2011015924

ISBN: 978-1-59702-027-5

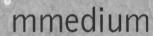

mmedium

inspiring a world of imagination

Sora and the Cloud

そら と くも

by Felicia Hoshino

フェリシャ 星野 / 作

Japanese translation
by Akiko Hisa

比佐 亜紀子 / 訳

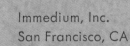

Immedium, Inc.
San Francisco, CA

こっちおいでー

Little Sora loves to climb.

小さな そらくんは のぼるのが だいすき。

おーい、あぶないぞー

As he grows, he climbs over everything in his path.

ずんずん 大きくなって、どんどん なんでも よじのぼっていっちゃう。

He even climbs people!

人だって のぼっちゃうぞ。ママも パパも！

Hooray, the playground! Big kid structures!

やったー こうえんだね！おっきい お兄ちゃんがのぼる ジャングルジムがあるよ。

たかいなー！

Then one day Sora climbs a tree. Up he climbs, higher and higher, as if there is no end.

ある日、そらくんは 木にのぼってみた。のぼっても のぼっても なかなか てっぺんには とどかない。

Peeking through the branches at the top, what does he find?

やっと いちばん上の こずえの間から のぞいてみた。何が見えたのかな？

A billowy cloud nestled in the leaves!

くもだ！はっぱの上で ふかふかのくもくんが 気持ちよさそうに おひるねしてる！

Cotton candy?
わたあめ
なのかなぁ?

Ahhh, so soft and fluffy!
Sora thinks of taking a bite when...

わー、やわらかくて ふわふわだ!
そらくんが ひとくち パクリと しようとした
その時・・・

Sora cannot resist climbing on to
the Cloud, waking it from its nap.

そらくんは ちょっと 目をさました くもくんに
どうしても のぼってみたくなった。

Suddenly Sora and the Cloud float up to the sky!
Everything below begins to shrink.

とつぜん、そらくんと くもくんは お空へふわり、とうかんだ！

ふたりの下に見えるものは だんだん 小さくなっていった。

Look! Ants!
みて！
アリさんだ！

"Where are we going?" Sora asks, but the Cloud
just sways side-to-side, winks, and then they both smile.

As Sora and the Cloud stroll above the streets, they head into the shadow of...

「ぼくたち　どこへ行くの？」
だけど くもくんは ただゆらーり、ゆらり。ウインクするから ふたりで くすっとわらった。

そらくんと くもくんが お空をふわふわ おさんぽしていると、だんだん かげに近づいて・・・

From way up in the sky, construction workers play with gigantic building blocks!

As Sora and the Cloud turn the corner, the sky lights up with the colors of...

高い、高い お空の上から見えるのは 工事のおじさんたち。ものすごく 大きな つみ木であそんでるよ！

そらくんと くもくんが 角をまがると、お空がいろんな色に ぴかぴか 光っていて・・・

From way up in the sky, rides spin and whirl in a kaleidoscope of motion!

As Sora and the Cloud soar by the sky glider, a gust of wind pulls them into...

高い、高い お空の上から見えるのは ゆうえんちの乗り物。万華鏡みたいに くるくる 回ってる。

そらくんと くもくんが ゴンドラのそばを さーっと飛ぶと、強い風が ふたりをぐいぐい 引っぱって・・・

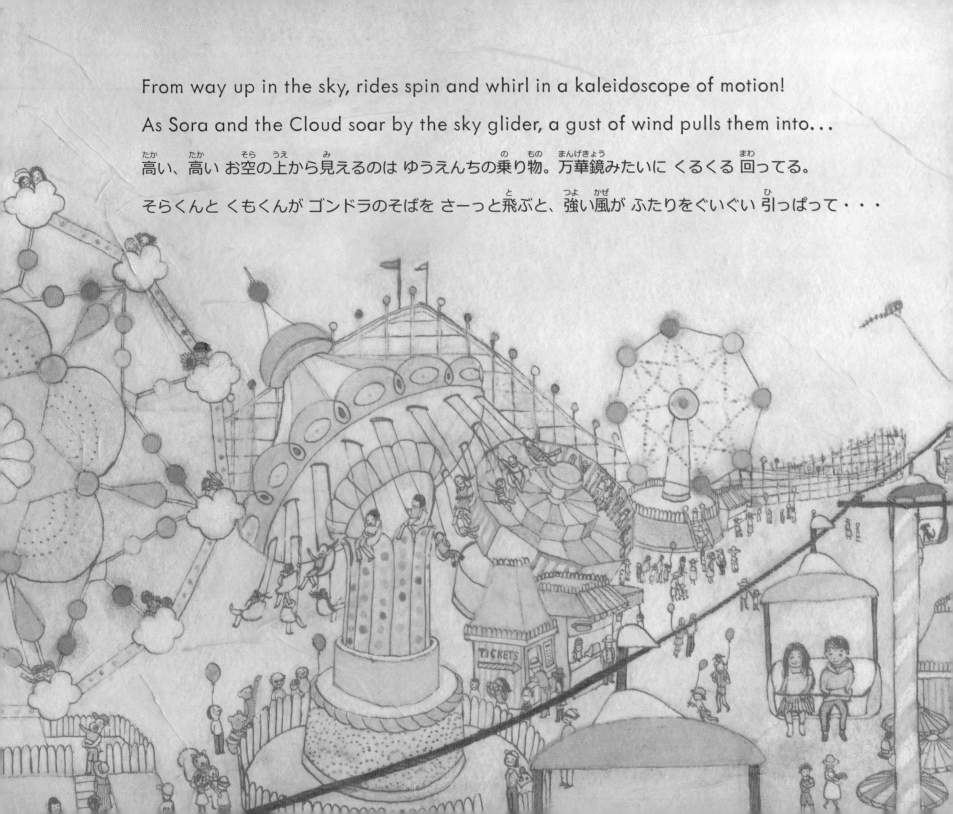

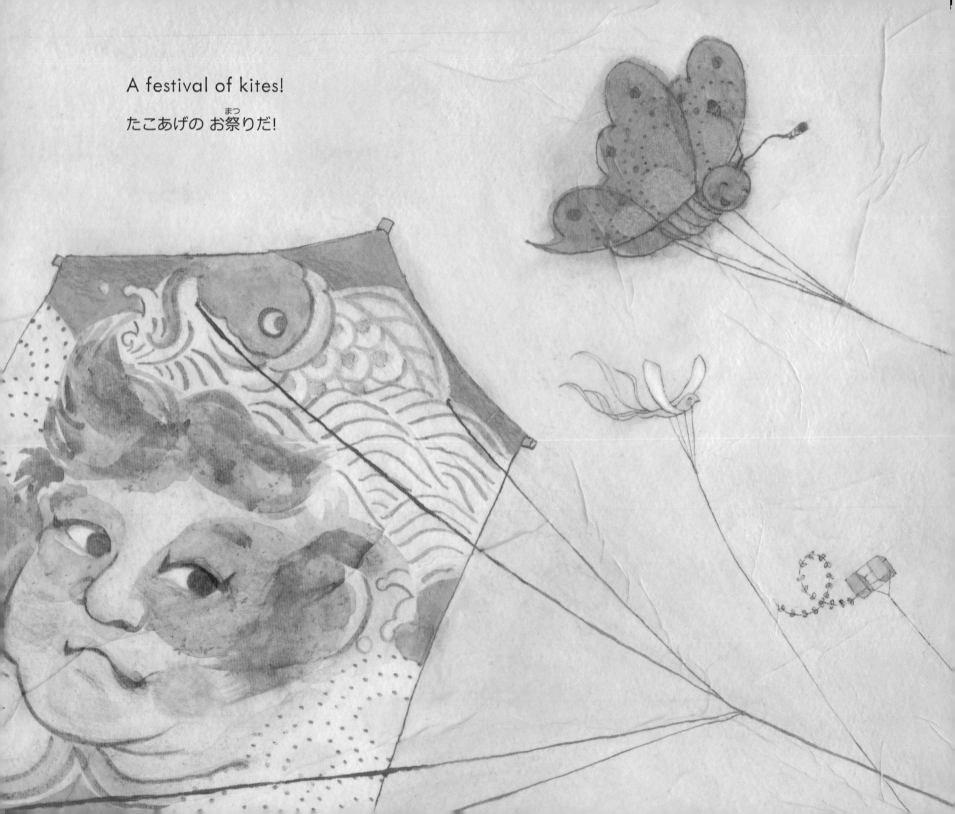

A festival of kites!

たこあげの お祭りだ!

From way up in the sky, kites swirl and squeal with delight.

As Sora and the Cloud weave through octopus tentacles and butterfly wings, the sky fills with the rumbling sound of...

高い、高い お空の上から見えるのは たこ。うれしそうに ぐるぐる きゅるきゅる 飛んでいる。

そらくんと くもくんが タコの足や チョウチョの羽の間を すいすい 飛ぶと、お空がぶるぶる 鳴っていて・・・

From way up in the sky, engines grrrowl and rooooaaarrr!

As Sora and the Cloud watch the airplane sprint away into the clouds,
the sky grows quiet and still...

高い、高い お空の上から聞こえてきたのは エンジンの音。ぐわおー！ぎゃおー！

そらくんと くもくんが 雲の中にぎゅーんと消えていく飛行機を見ていると、

そのうちお空は しーんと 静かになって・・・

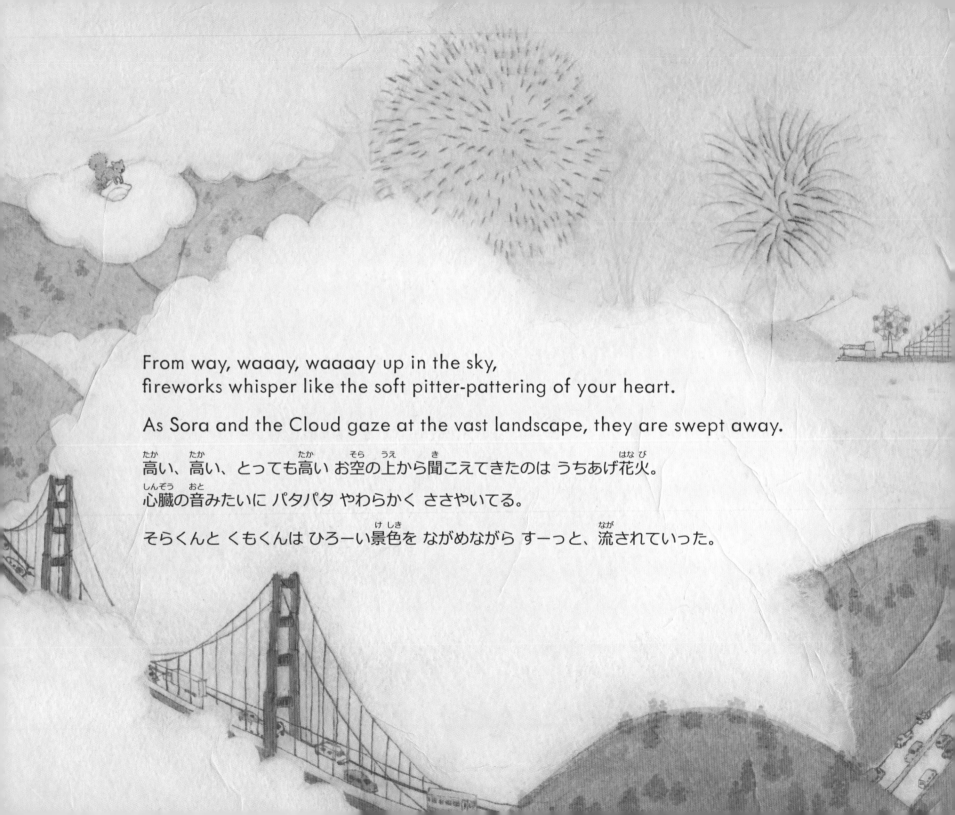

From way, waaay, waaaay up in the sky,
fireworks whisper like the soft pitter-pattering of your heart.

As Sora and the Cloud gaze at the vast landscape, they are swept away.

高い、高い、とっても高い お空の上から 聞こえてきたのは うちあげ花火。

心臓の音みたいに パタパタ やわらかく ささやいてる。

そらくんと くもくんは ひろーい景色を ながめながら すーっと、流されていった。

きをつけてー！

Like a mobile in the breeze, Sora's sky adventure spins all around him.

Slowly, Sora and the Cloud drift gently to sleep and down to earth.

そよ風にゆれる モビールみたいに、そらくんの お空のぼうけんは くるくる くるん と回ってる。

そらくんと くもくんは うとうと しながら、ゆっくり 地面におりていった。

As grey clouds gather and raindrops tickle his face...

灰色の雲が集まると、雨つぶが そらくんの顔を こちょこちょ くすぐって・・・

Sora dreams of splashing in big puddles.

そらくんは 水たまりで バシャバシャ あそぶ夢をみた。

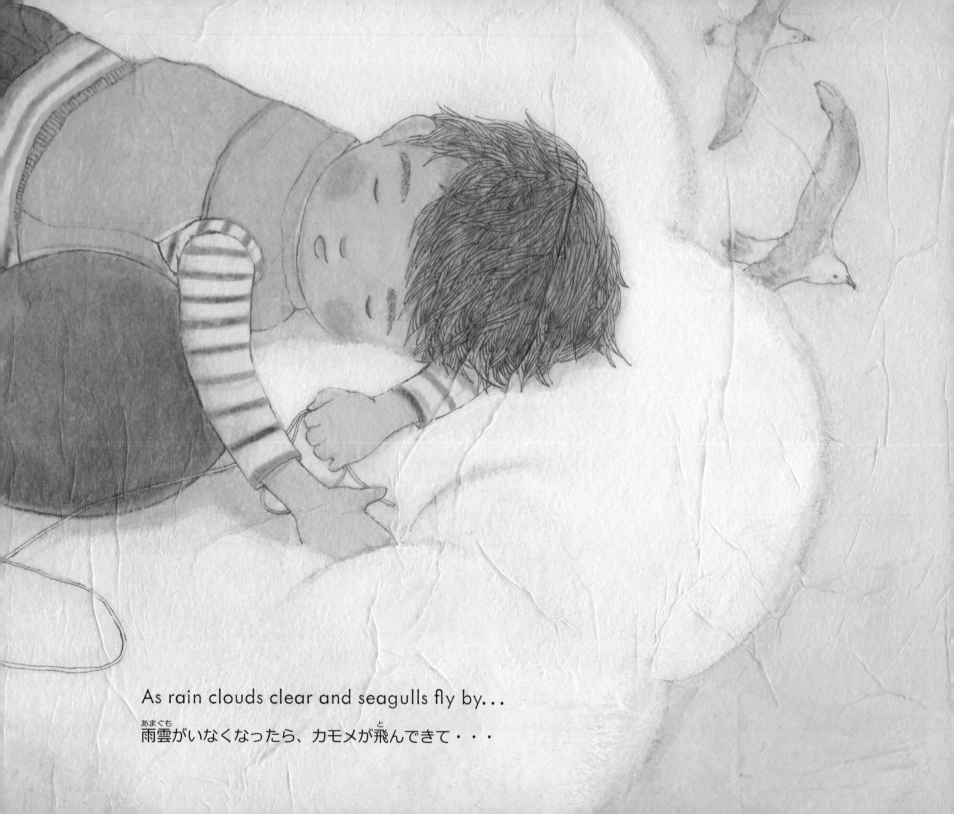

As rain clouds clear and seagulls fly by...

雨雲がいなくなったら、カモメが飛んできて・・・

Sora dreams of digging in wet sand.

それから 海岸のお砂をほっている 夢をみた。

As the sun shines through and its rays warm his body...

雨あがりのおひさまは きらきらして そらくんの体を ぽかぽか あたためると・・・

Sora dreams of napping on a bed of grass.

草のベッドで おひるねをする 夢を見た。

Sora and the Cloud dream.

そらくんと くもくんは ふたりでいっしょに 夢を見た。

"Where are we going next time?" Sora asks, but the Cloud
just sways side-to-side, winks, and then they both smile.

As Sora climbs down the tree, he can't wait to tell his little sister
about his new friend the Cloud.

「今度 会うときは どこにいこうか？」
そらくんは くもくんに聞いてみた。だけど くもくんは ただゆらーり、ゆらり。ウインクするだけ。
そしてふたりで くすっと わらった。

そらくんは 木からおりながら いもうとに あたらしいともだちの くもくんのことを話すのが
すごくまちどおしかった。

こんにちわー

Note to Readers

I wanted *Sora and the Cloud* to be bilingual, simply so that both my husband and I could enjoy reading it to our children in each of our native languages; for myself in English and for my husband in Japanese. I also wanted to include the following notes to introduce English readers, (myself included) to Japanese expressions and cultural elements that were inspirational to the storyline and illustrations.

Special Thanks

To Mom, Dad, Yoshi, Sora, Yume, Akiko, Chiaki, and Oliver for your inspiration, support, and patience. – Felicia

To Felipe, Noriko, and Takemi for your kind hearts. – Akiko

Glossary

Sora そら / 空 : means "sky"
Kumo くも / 雲 : means "cloud"

Japanese Cultural Inspirations

Japanese Short Expressions

pg 1 - grandmother to Sora こっちおいでー
(kocchi oide) : Come this way

pg 2 - grandfather to Sora おーい、あぶないぞー
(ooi, abunaizo) : Hey, watch it

pg 3 - mother to Sora こら！ (kora) : Hey! Excuse you!

pg 3 - father to Sora いててー (itete) : Ouch

pg 4 - Sora to mother みてみてー！ (mite mite) : Look at me!

pg 4 - mother to Sora きをつけてー！ (ki wo tsukete) : Be careful!

pg 5 - Sora to tree たかいなー！ (takaina) : Wow, so tall!

pg 20 - Sora to fireworks すごーい！ (sugoi) : Wow, great!

pg 21 - mother to Sora きをつけてー！ (ki wo tsukete) : Be careful!

pg 28 - little sister to butterfly チョウチョ！ (choucho) : Butterfly!

pg 30 - Sora to Cloud (in bubble) くもくん、ありがとうね。
(Kumo-kun arigatou ne) : Thank you Cloud

pg 31 - little sister to Cloud こんにちわー (konnichiwa) : Hello

Note - The dash "ー" (chouon) is used to extend the vowel sound that comes before it.

pg 13 - Takoyaki (たこやき)

Food booths are commonly found at festivals in Japan. Originated in Osaka, *takoyaki* is a ball shaped dumpling made of wheat batter with a tiny piece of octopus 蛸 (*tako*) inside.

pg 15 - Kintaro (きんたろう / 金太郎)

A Japanese boy hero painted on many kites. He grows up to be a very strong man. This kite represents strength, endurance, and valor and would be given to a boy on his birthday.

pg 16 - Tako tako agare (たこ たこ あがれ)

Translates into "Kites are rising in the sky," lyrics to the classic children's song "Tako no Uta." In Japanese, the word *tako* (pronounced *taco*) has two meanings: octopus 蛸 and kite 凧.

pg 18 - Shishimai (ししまい / 獅子舞)

A traditional Japanese lion dance performed to celebrate the new year. The airplane's face is inspired by the wooden head of the lion dance costume.

More books by Felicia Hoshino

My Dog Teny written by Yoshito Wayne Osaki
2011 Society of Illustrators "Original Art"

A Place Where Sunflowers Grow written by Amy Lee-Tai
2007 Jane Addams Peace Award

2007 Society of Illustrators "Original Art"

2007 International Reading Association
Children's Book Award - Notable

2007 Notable Books for a Global Society

2007 ForeWord Book of the Year Finalist

Bloomsbury Reviews Favorite Reads of 2006

San Francisco Chronicle Best Books of the Season Pick 2006

Little Sap and Monsieur Rodin written by Michelle Lord

Bank Street College Children's Book Committee
Children's Books of the Year

2007 Society of Illustrators "Original Art"

Finding the Golden Ruler written by Karen Hill

Surprise Moon written by Caroline Hatton

www.felishino.com

Part of this book's proceeds go to Japan Earthquake Relief.